APARTHEID

Racial Segregation in South Africa

Written by Marie Fauré
In collaboration with Magali Bailliot
Translated by Rebecca Neal

History **50**MINUTES.com

APARTHEID

KEY INFORMATION

- **When:** 1948-1991.
- **Where:** South Africa.
- **Context:** the rise to power of Afrikaner nationalists.
- **Key protagonists:**
  ○ Daniel Malan, South African politician (1874-1959).
  ○ Nelson Mandela, South African lawyer and statesman (1918-2013).
  ○ F.W. de Klerk, South African statesman (born in 1936).
- **Impact:**
  ○ The restoration of democracy in South Africa.
  ○ The election of Nelson Mandela as President of South Africa in 1994.

INTRODUCTION

The apartheid regime is undoubtedly one of the most significant events of the second half of the 20th century. For those who lived through it, this period left a major impression and cannot be separated from Nelson Mandela, the man who symbolised its fall and who became one of the most important representatives of the fight against racism. The segregation that South Africa's non-white population endured in this period is shocking because of its cruelty and duration, as well as its international impact.

'Apartheid' is an Afrikaans word meaning 'separateness' or 'the state of being apart' (literally 'apart-hood'). It refers to a policy of 'separate development', in which different populations are kept in particular geographical areas based on ethnic or linguistic criteria. This policy was implemented by the National Party in 1948, with the aid of laws and rules which sought to regulate the relationships between white and non-white populations in South Africa in order to ensure the economic, social and political domination of the former over the latter. There were two types of apartheid, known as petty apartheid, which governed everyday contact in the public sphere, and grand apartheid, which aimed to create separated, ethnically determined geographical zones.

As such, until the system was abolished in 1991, South African society was based on an official regime of racial segregation, in spite of increasing international condemnation and violently repressed opposition, symbolised by the African National Congress (ANC) and one of its charismatic leaders, Nelson Mandela. Although the country successfully transitioned to nonracial democracy, South Africa now faces a number of economic and social challenges.

CONTEXT

SOUTH AFRICA: COLONISATION AND RIVALRIES

The colonisation of South Africa began in 1652 with the creation of Cape Colony by the Dutch East India Company. Dutch Calvinist immigrants flocked to this new territory, where they were gradually joined by other Calvinists from France, Germany, Scandinavia and the Republic of the Seven United Netherlands (the northern part of the present-day Netherlands). From the beginning, these white populations, who were called Afrikaners, were afraid of being lost in the crowd of the pre-existing black Bantu population. For this reason, a strong Afrikaner identity took shape, based on a language (Afrikaans), a religion (Calvinism) and activities such as slave trading and the use of slaves in farming. This identity-based position was strengthened with the arrival of the British, who the Afrikaners viewed unfavourably, in the 19th century. This solidified their nationalism, which was then presented as a movement of resistance against British oppression. The doctrine of this nationalism was based on the idea that the Afrikaners were a chosen people, destined to rule the land occupied by the first colonisers.

However, Cape Colony was definitively handed over to the British Crown in 1814, and the English were quick to establish cultural and political hegemony. They even went so far as to directly attack Afrikaner identity by removing Afrikaans as a national language in 1822, and to jeopardise their economy by abolishing slavery in 1833. The abolition of slavery drove

14 000 Afrikaners to leave the coastal regions and head inland (the Great Trek, 1835-1840) to create independent republics north of Cape Town, in particular the Transvaal and the Orange Free Street.

The situation deteriorated during the second half of the 19th century, following the establishment of a British colonial settlement and a major seizure of land. This led directly to the Boer War (1899-1902) and the creation of the Union of South Africa in 1910, which brought the Afrikaner republics together under British control. In spite of attempts at compromise between the British and the Afrikaners, the ideological and economic differences between them remained pronounced. While the Afrikaners had tried to control the local populations by segregation since their arrival, the British had entirely different ideas. Indeed, once they had been converted to Christianity by evangelising missions, the indigenous inhabitants were considered to be subjects of the Crown. This was unthinkable for the Afrikaners, who saw the native peoples as nothing more than a servile workforce. Furthermore, the Afrikaners harboured a great deal of resentment towards the British, who had been responsible for thousands of deaths during the Boer War. This feeling was reinforced by the ethnic mixing that occurred as a result of the mining industry.

Within this context of heightened Afrikaner nationalism, the arrival of so-called 'Coloured' populations consolidated the bases of the future policy. The Afrikaners felt trapped between the English-speaking middle class and the indigenous and immigrant workforce. In addition, Afrikaner independence projects resurfaced in the postwar period. The concept of Afrikanerdom put forward by Paul Kruger (South African statesman, 1825-1904), which was a political project for the creation of a wholly Afrikaner area of land, made a comeback, and the term 'apartheid' was used for the first time by Jan Smuts (South African statesman, 1870-1950) in a 1917 speech.

OMNIPRESENT RACIAL SEGREGATION

In practice, an increasing number of regulations were applied to the black populations even prior to apartheid. Cape Colony implemented Pass Laws starting in 1809 and established geographical zones with the Glen Grey Act in 1894. Some even recommended the creation of indigenous reserves, which would function as reservoirs of workers for the white population.

The policy of racial segregation was strengthened with the creation of the Union of South Africa. Non-white populations were not allowed to vote, and interracial relationships were increasingly controlled. The 1911 Native Labour Regulation Act established racial barriers at work, while the 1913 Native Land Act forbade black South Africans from owning land outside the reserves. Finally, the Native Urban Areas Act in 1923 officially established urban spatial segregation.

In the face of this injustice, a form of resistance appeared. This resistance took shape through protest actions and the creation of organisations and trade unions, including the South African Native National Congress in 1912, which became the ANC in 1923. Initially an intellectual organisation which struggled to impose itself, the ANC was reshaped as a mass party in 1943-1944 and created a Youth League at the instigation of Nelson Mandela in particular, which quickly became radicalised.

THE CONTRADICTIONS OF SOUTH AFRICA AT THE END OF THE SECOND WORLD WAR

At the end of the Second World War, South Africa had a stake in the new world order. It joined the United Nations (UN) on 7 November 1945 and became a founding member of UNESCO in November 1946. And yet, one of the goals of the UN is to fight against racism and intolerance, which are condemned in the constitution that South Africa helped to write.

For this reason, the government at the time announced a relaxation of the racial policy, the recognition of the rights of every individual, whatever their skin colour, and the exercise of citizenship for all. However, as the urban black population was much larger than the white population, this strengthened the nationalism of the Afrikaners. The consequences of this were not long in coming, and the 1948 elections brought the National Party under Daniel Malan to power. From there, the National Party were able to establish apartheid.

DID YOU KNOW?

At the start of apartheid, the South African population

was:

- 67% black;
- 21% white (of these, 60% were Afrikaners and 40% were English speakers);
- 9% mixed ethnicity (this group was labelled 'Coloured');
- <3% Indians (from Asia).

KEY PROTAGONISTS

DANIEL MALAN, CALVINIST PREACHER AND SOUTH AFRICAN POLITICIAN

Portrait of Daniel Malan

Daniel Malan was born in Cape Colony in 1874 to a white family of French origin. He grew up on the family farm with a father who was a fervent supporter of Calvinism and Afrikaner identity. Malan was initially a preacher in the Protestant Church. A brilliant speaker, he gradually established himself as one of the central figures of Afrikaner nationalism in the first half of the 20th century. He was a Darwinist and a great defender of the unity of the Afrikaner people, who he saw as a people who had been chosen by God and were destined to impose their will on the indigenous populations. He became head of government in 1948 and was the instigator of apartheid.

He retired from politics in 1954 and died five years later.

NELSON MANDELA, SOUTH AFRICAN LAWYER AND STATESMAN

Portrait of Nelson Mandela

Born in the poor village of Mzevo in the Transkei (south-east South Africa, the first independent Bantustan under the apartheid regime) in 1918, Nelson Mandela entered politics in 1943. Along with two other activists, he founded the Youth League of the ANC one year later, and in 1961 he became leader of the new armed branch of the organisation, Umkhonto we Sizwe (Xhosa for 'Spear of the Nation').

Mandela was arrested in 1962 for retaliation against the violent repression of peaceful campaigning and sentenced to life in prison. He was freed on 11 February 1990 on the orders of the new South African president F.W. de Klerk. He played an active part in the negotiations which led to the abolition of apartheid and the drawing up of a provisional constitution, which earned him the Nobel Peace Prize in 1993.

On 27 April 1994, he was elected as the first black president in the history of South Africa, thus becoming the leader of the 'Rainbow Nation' – a term used by Archbishop Desmond Tutu to characterise the hope and beauty of the country at this time – until the end of his term in 1999. A symbol of the fight against racism, Mandela continued to defend democracy, equality and knowledge across the world. In 1999, he established the Nelson Mandela Foundation, which aims to preserve and analyse the past in order to promote freedom and equality for all.

His death on 5 December 2013 inspired intense emotion, and tributes poured in from all over the world. Since 2009, Mandela Day has been celebrated on 18 July, his birthday. This day was established by the UN with the aim of honouring his life and continuing his fight.

F.W. DE KLERK, SOUTH AFRICAN STATESMAN

Portrait of F.W. de Klerk

F.W. de Klerk was born in Johannesburg in 1936 and is the son of a South African politician. He studied law and became a lawyer. He was elected to Parliament for the National Party in 1972, then occupied a series of ministerial posts from 1978 onwards. A staunch conservative, he displayed unstinting support for the application of apartheid.

However, when he was elected leader of the National Party in February 1989, and against all expectations, de Klerk spoke for the first time in favour of a South Africa free from racial segregation, perhaps with the aim of putting an end to years of violence and the country's isolation on the international scene. He was elected president in August of the same year, and was behind the negotiations which ended the policy of apartheid and paved the way for the introduction of a new constitution for the country. He shared the 1993 Nobel Peace Prize with Nelson Mandela, who he had freed three years earlier. He became vice-president under Mandela in 1994, before withdrawing from politics three years later. He then set up the F.W. de Klerk Foundation, which aims to preserve the legacy of his political activity by defending the constitution and promoting diversity in South Africa.

APARTHEID

SETTING UP A REGIME OF SEGREGATION

The victory of the National Party, which was linked to the Afrikaner Party, in 1948, marked the implementation of apartheid, which now formed part of government policy. Fearing an uprising from the African peoples, the measures put in place aimed to fix the relationships between the different races and population groups, and only granted democratic rights to white people.

First of all, the policy involved limiting contact between the different communities. This was achieved by identifying populations based on their racial and ethnic affiliation and organising them into five classes as described in the 1950 Population Registration Act: whites, Bantus (black people from central and southern Africa), Zulus (the Bantu population of South Africa), Indians (from Asia) and Coloured (those of mixed race). Laws governing everyday behaviour and social relationships were also implemented. As such, interracial marriage was banned from 1949 and interracial sexual relations were outlawed a year later.

The new regime also drew up the Group Areas Act, which geographically defined apartheid. Through this law, the white leaders were able to rationalise urban segregation to an extreme degree by designating residential and activity zones for each social group that were exclusive to them. In this way, townships (poor and underequipped zones situated on the outskirts of towns and cities and reserved for non-whites) were created. These neighbourhoods, which were made up of makeshift houses and had no real amenities, were separated from other urban spaces by buffer zones, and their rare points of contact were controlled by the forces of law and order, with black populations needing pass books to move around.

Photograph of a shop on the main street of a township in South Africa.

Sign indicating that the beach and its facilities are for white people only.

At the same time, the government tried to exclude the Indian and Coloured populations from the common electoral roll by creating separate electoral colleges. However, in the face of strong opposition from Parliament and the declaration by the Supreme Court that it was invalid, this law was finally repealed in 1956.

When Hendrik Verwoerd (South African politician, 1901-1966) became Minister for Native Affairs in 1951, the Bantu Authorities Act was introduced. This organised the way things would be run for Bantus (the black population in South Africa) by establishing tribal authorities which depended entirely on the government, encouraging corruption and cronyism, and by defining their areas of territory (Bantustans). In this way, ten Bantustans were created, bringing together the black population, who were at the time the majority in South Africa, in only 13% of the territory. The land they were granted was not suitable for agriculture and lacked resources and industry. This law was complemented by the 1959 Promotion of Bantu Self-Government Act, which granted the Bantustans a greater degree of autonomy, and the Black Homeland Citizenship Act in 1970, which forcibly gave all black South Africans citizenship of one of the Bantustans, whether they lived there or not, thus stripping them of their South African nationality. The Transkei was the first Bantustan to acquire self-government in 1963, then independence in 1976. It was followed in this by Bophuthatswana in 1977, Venda in 1979 and Ciskei in 1981. In total, an estimated 3.5 million black South Africans were forcibly displaced during apartheid.

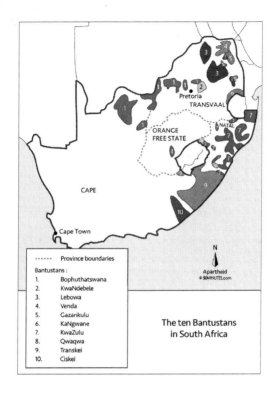

Province boundaries

Bantustans :
1. Bophuthatswana
2. KwaNdebele
3. Lebowa
4. Venda
5. Gazankulu
6. KaNgwane
7. KwaZulu
8. Qwaqwa
9. Transkei
10. Ciskei

Apartheid
© 50MINUTES.com

The ten Bantustans
in South Africa

On the basis of these laws, the regime became stricter during the 1980s, intensifying their repression and violence against the increasingly aggressive resistance movements of the populations.

THE MAIN LAWS OF APARTHEID

- 1949: Prohibition of Mixed Marriages Act (which outlawed interracial marriage)
- 1950: Immorality Amendment Act (which outlawed sexual relationships between whites and non-whites); Population Registration Act (which classified populations according to their ethnic affiliation); Group Areas Act (which separated the urban areas that each group could live in); Separate Representation of Voters Act (which established a separate electoral roll for Coloured citizens); Suppression of Communism Act (which outlawed any political parties affiliated with Communism)
- 1951: Bantu Authorities Act (which organised a separate political system in the reserves)
- 1952: Native Abolition of Passes and Coordination Documents Act (which dealt with the need for black citizens over the age of 16 to carry pass books); Native Laws Amendment Act (which limited the right of black South Africans to live in the cities)
- 1953: Reservation of Separation of Amenities Act (which dealt with the use of public facilities); Bantu Education Act (which established the segregation of Bantus in all schools); Native Labour [Settlement of Disputes] Act (which forbade black workers from going on strike)
- 1954: Native Resettlement Act (which organised the resettlement of indigenous peoples living in white areas)

- 1956: Industrial Conciliation Act (which encouraged racial discrimination at work)
- 1959: Extension of University Education Act (which established universities exclusive to black, Indian and Coloured citizens); Promotion of Bantu Self-Government Act (which dealt with the self-government of the Bantustans)
- 1970: Black Homeland Citizenship Act (which stripped the black population of South African citizenship)

SOUTH AFRICAN RESISTANCE

Resistance to apartheid mainly came from the black community. Initially, this resistance took the form of political campaigning. In 1949, the ANC adopted the Programme of Action, a strategy of demanding rights based on non-violence and civil disobedience. It was put into action in 1952 with a campaign calling on citizens to deliberately and peacefully transgress the laws of apartheid.

AN EXAMPLE OF PROTEST

In 1957, to protest against the sudden fare increase on buses between the township and the centre of Johannesburg 10 km away, the population of Alexandra won their case by boycotting public transport and travelling by foot for months.

In order to clarify the claims of Coloured and black citizens, representatives from the ANC, the South African Indian Congress, the South African Congress of Democrats and the Federation of South African Women met in 1955 and drew up the Freedom Charter. In particular, they demanded equal rights and the end of racial discrimination. The government strongly opposed this initiative and had members of the ANC arrested for treason. They were acquitted in 1961.

As their demands had still not been heard, the campaigners took further action, including the peaceful protest against the fact that black citizens had to carry pass books which took place in Sharpeville on 21 March 1960. On that day, the protestors all voluntarily went to the police station in the township with the aim of being arrested for failing to carry a pass book. So many people participated that the police were soon overwhelmed and had to call in reinforcements. When one of the policemen stumbled, the crowd rushed forward and the police began to fire on them. 69 protestors were killed and a further 180 were injured. In Cape Town, the population of the Langa township responded to this repression by burning public buildings. The government then declared a state of emergency and outlawed the ANC and the Pan-Africanist Congress, forcing the resistance underground. In the face of this violence, an armed branch of the ANC, Umkhonto we Sizwe (MK) was formed in 1961 and immediately embarked on a campaign of sabotaging official buildings. The movement's leaders, including Nelson Mandela, were soon arrested and sentenced to life imprisonment.

Photograph taken in 1960 of Nelson Mandela burning a pass book.

Protests continued, and on 16 June 1976 the Soweto uprising took place. This was followed by a major campaign of violence and repression. On the day of the uprising, a law forcing pupils to use Afrikaans at school had just been approved by the national authorities and students decided to protest in the streets of the township of Soweto. Once again, the police responded with brutality, leading to the deaths of multiple protestors. Weeks of riots, boycotts, strikes and mass demonstrations ensued, while MK carried out an increasing number of attacks, leading to the implementation of martial law.

Photograph of a student carrying the lifeless body of Hector Pieterson.

On New Year's Day 1985, Olivier Tambo (anti-apartheid activist, 1917-1993) called on Radio Freedom listeners to make the country impossible to govern. One year later, 54 townships had embarked on all-out war. The situation was entirely beyond the control of the authorities, and the president Pieter Botha (1916-2006) declared a state of emergency and sent the army into the townships. Police violence became an everyday occurrence.

INTERNATIONAL CONDEMNATION

As of 1950, the United Nations Commission on Human Rights condemned segregation in South Africa, and three years later UNESCO asked the government to reconsider its policy. However, the country's only response was to withdraw from the organisation in late 1956.

The voices speaking out against apartheid became louder after the Sharpeville massacre in 1960. The UN Security Council condemned the killing, as did the Commonwealth, of which South Africa was a member. In the face of this criticism, the government withdrew from the Commonwealth in 1961 and proclaimed the country the independent Republic of South Africa.

In spite of South Africa's flat refusal to alter its policy, the UN continued to act against the apartheid regime. A Special Committee was set up in 1963, and the UN called on states to suspend all sales of arms and oil to South Africa. The country was excluded from the World Health Organisation, the International Labour Organisation and the International Olympic Committee. In 1973, the UN General Assembly ratified the International Convention on the Suppression and Punishment of the Crime of Apartheid, which classified the segregationist regime as a crime against humanity.

The Soweto uprising in 1976 and the resulting explosion of violence profoundly shocked international opinion. When the regime adopted an even tougher stance, international condemnation became more restrictive and economically challenging for the country. While the UN refused to recognise the Transkei as an independent state – an approach it would follow for the other Bantustans – in 1977 it made the arms embargo obligatory. During the 1980s, an increasing number of sanctions were imposed and took the form of diplomatic and trade restrictions. As such, Sweden, Denmark and Norway decreed a complete embargo on trade with South Africa, while the USA passed the Comprehensive Anti-Apartheid Act in 1986, which halted all investment and trade exchanges for as long as apartheid remained in place. This had a major impact on the South African economy, in spite of the country's attempts to bypass the restrictions.

During this decade, public opinion rallied to demand the release of Nelson Mandela, who had become the symbol of the anti-apartheid fight. In particular, there were an increasing number of songs and concerts of support in his honour.

NELSON MANDELA: A KEY FIGURE IN THE FIGHT AGAINST APARTHEID

During his imprisonment on Robben Island and then in Pollsmoor Prison in Cape Town, Nelson Mandela worked tirelessly towards the goal he had set himself, and which he clearly expressed on 20 April 1964 at the end of the trial of the leaders of the armed wing of the ANC: "I have cherished the ideal of a democratic and free society in which all persons live together in harmony and with equal opportunities. It is an ideal which I hope to live for and to achieve. But if needs be, it is an appeal for which I am prepared to die" (Nelson Mandela Foundation, 2011). For this reason, he honed his skills as a lawyer and studied the history and language of the Afrikaners, as he thought that it was necessary to know his opponents in order to build peace together.

He continued his mission and repeatedly refused to submit to the conditions imposed by the South African government in exchange for his freedom. His personal sacrifice for the benefit of his cause won him the admiration of the entire world.

THE LONG PROCESS OF ABOLISHING APARTHEID

Amid increasingly brutal repression in South Africa, Pieter Botha softened legal persecution, although without altering the two fundamental laws of apartheid, the Population Registration Act and the Group Areas Act. He gradually restored rights to the non-white population, in particular by abolishing jobs reserved for certain groups, pass books and the rules against interracial marriage. He also opened public spaces to all communities. Furthermore, interracial trade unions and non-white political parties were legalised again, provided that they had not been banned in the past, which excluded the ANC. In order to get around this law, the black opposition founded the Congress of South African Trade Unions (COSATU). However, faced with an increase in violence and strike action, the government reversed this decision and once again restricted black organisations in the country.

In 1984, Botha announced a new constitution, which granted the semblance of political rights to Indian and Coloured citizens, in particular through the creation of separate Houses in a Tricameral Parliament. At the same time, the constitution strengthened the militarisation of the regime and the power of the president, which is why it was rejected by the UN.

In the general climate of insurrection, secret talks began between Nelson Mandela and the South African president, but these would have very limited success until F.W. de Klerk, who wanted to end apartheid, came to power in 1989. Although de Klerk was initially a conservative, at the start of 1989 he publicly stated his opinion that South Africa could not continue with this policy and that negotiations must take place. He was supported in this by the UN, which adopted a resolution on 14 December 1989 calling for negotiations in order to end apartheid and put in place a nonracial democracy. In a speech on 2 February 1990, de Klerk announced to the world the lifting of the ban on the ANC and the political parties, the suspension of the death penalty and the state of emergency, and the authorisation of trade union activity and the release of political prisoners. He also paved the way for the first multiracial democratic elections in the country. Through this speech and the release of Nelson Mandela on 11 February, de Klerk sent a strong signal to South Africa and the rest of the world, and in May he officially began negotiations with the ANC. This led to the definitive suspension of the armed conflict in August. One year later, in June 1991, the founding laws of the apartheid regime were abolished.

IMPACT

THE RESTORATION OF DEMOCRACY IN SOUTH AFRICA

The abolition of the laws of apartheid was only the beginning of a long process leading to the drawing up of a new constitution and the holding of multiracial elections.

A Convention for a Democratic South Africa (CODESA) was held in Johannesburg at the end of 1991 and brought together delegates from the 19 parties representing the different provinces and ethnic groups. The aim of the convention was to establish negotiations leading to the drafting of a new constitution. Although a referendum held in March 1992 gave de Klerk a mandate to negotiate this new text with the ANC, the inflexibility of the National Party posed a serious threat to the convention. Consequently, at Mandela's request, the UN put in place an observation mission on 17 August 1992 with the aim of helping the country to suppress violence and ensure that the negotiations ran smoothly. The interim constitution was finally adopted on 18 November 1993. Having observed an improvement in the situation, the UN lifted international economic sanctions.

Nelson Mandela and F.W. de Klerk shake hands during the 1992 World Economic Forum.

Although violence in the townships in the weeks before the election, which far-right Afrikaners claimed credit for, led many to fear the worst, no major problems arose on the big day. The polls brought the ANC and Nelson Mandela to power. Upon his election, Mandela established a government of national unity represented by his two vice-presidents, F.W. de Klerk of the National Party and Thabo Mbeki (born in 1942) of the ANC. The new constitution, published in May 1996, led to the resignation of National Party ministers. On an economic and social level, the government implemented a Reconstruction and Development Programme in 1994. However, over twenty years after the introduction of these measures, the results remain mixed, with democratic success but persistent inequality.

SOUTH AFRICA TODAY

Since then, South Africa has become the economic driving force of the African continent. At the end of the 2000s, 158 of its companies were listed among the top 500 companies in the world. These companies alone represent over 51% of the continent's revenue. For all that, although the transition to democracy has been successful, South African society has struggled to eradicate the consequences of apartheid, and inequality persists. Whites have retained their stranglehold over land, which causes major social tensions. The average income of black South Africans is eight times lower than that of white South Africans, and almost 45% of the population lives on under 2 dollars per day.

Furthermore, inequalities remain quite visible on the geographical level: the majority of black South Africans still live in townships, even after the disappearance of the Bantustans. The inhabitants of the townships feel excluded from the South African 'miracle' and betrayed by the ANC, which has led to new uprisings. On 16 August 2012, the police responded to a miners' strike in Marikana with violence, killing 34 demonstrators and injuring a further 78. Some inequalities therefore persist, and the re-election of Thabo Mbeki as president in 2004 did not change this.

Ultimately, there are two possible readings of the country's post-apartheid track record. The first, favoured by liberals, recognises the partial success of the regime thanks to the success of the transition to democracy. The second reading underlines the continuities with the apartheid regime that are visible on the socio-economic level in some parts of the country. As such, although South Africa has now found a certain degree of stability, there are still many difficulties to overcome.

A DUTY TO REMEMBER?

In 1995, Nelson Mandela used the Promotion of National Unity and Reconciliation Act to set up a commission to take an inventory of the human rights violations committed by supporters and opponents of apartheid between 1960 and 1993, in order to move on from the past and build a new, healthy society. This Truth and Reconciliation Commission was led by Desmond Tutu, the first black Archbishop of Cape Town, who used the accounts of both victims and per-petrators to try to understand the past while restoring the dignity of the victims. Finally, the commission was given the power to grant amnesties to those who requested them.

Nevertheless, the intentions of the commission were not received well. Whereas white South Africans did not see the need to go back over the past and were worried that scores would be settled, the victims of apartheid were frustrated that those who had persecuted them would be granted amnesty and thereby avoid being brought to justice. For this reason, in April 1996, the victims began a lawsuit which challenged the legality of the commission.

Defining how the memory of apartheid should be preserved is no easy task. Two opposing approaches soon emerged. The first can be represented by the Apartheid Museum, created by the government in 2001 and situated between

Johannesburg and Soweto. It aims to inspire strong emotions in visitors as they come face to face with segregation and oppression, before reassuring them thanks to the fall of the regime and the measures taken to abolish segregation. The second approach is represented by the District Six Museum, founded in 1989 by the former inhabitants of this neighbourhood which was declared white in 1962 but would remain multiethnic until its destruction in 1982. It aims to illustrate the social bonds that apartheid destroyed, the effects of which are still visible today.

Although South Africa has now rediscovered a certain degree of political and economic stability, it will be a long time before the wounds that apartheid inflicted in the hearts and minds of its citizens are fully healed.

SUMMARY

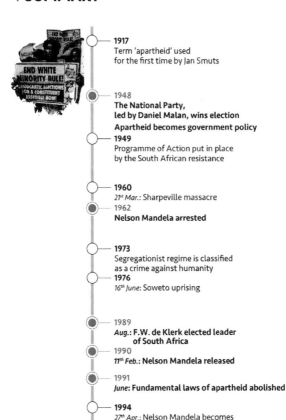

1917
Term 'apartheid' used
for the first time by Jan Smuts

1948
**The National Party,
led by Daniel Malan, wins election
Apartheid becomes government policy**

1949
Programme of Action put in place
by the South African resistance

1960
21st Mar.: Sharpeville massacre

1962
Nelson Mandela arrested

1973
Segregationist regime is classified
as a crime against humanity

1976
16th June: Soweto uprising

1989
Aug.: **F.W. de Klerk elected leader
of South Africa**

1990
11th Feb.: **Nelson Mandela released**

1991
June: **Fundamental laws of apartheid abolished**

1994
27th Apr.: Nelson Mandela becomes
the first black president of South Africa

Apartheid © 50MINUTES.com

- In 1948, the National Party won the South African elections. In 1950, the party implemented the first laws imposing segregation: the Population Registration Act, which classified the population by race, and the Group Areas Act, which initiated spatial segregation based on race.
- In 1951, the Bantu Authorities Act created Bantustans, geographical areas reserved for the black population. This law was reinforced by the Promotion of Bantu Self-Government Act in 1959 and the Homeland Citizenship Act in 1970, which turned the Bantustans into independent territories that each black person had to hold nationality for. This meant that they all lost their South African nationality.
- On 20 March 1960, the police killed 69 protestors in Sharpeville. After the violent response of the black opposition, the ANC was banned and forced underground. Its leaders, including Nelson Mandela, were arrested in the following years.
- One year later, as it faced international criticism, the South African government proclaimed the independent Republic of South Africa, which allowed the country to withdraw from the Commonwealth.
- In 1973, the apartheid regime was recognised as a crime against humanity by the UN.
- On 16 June 1976, the police fired on students demonstrating in Soweto. This led to several weeks of riots and brutal repression. After this new incident, international bodies adopted harsher measures against South Africa.
- In 1978, Pieter Botha became prime minister and then president. He removed some legal persecution, but

strengthened repression. When a new constitution was presented in 1984, it was rejected by the UN.

- On 1 January 1985, following an appeal issued on the radio, the townships rose up against the government. For months, the country was in a state of insurrection, and the situation was completely beyond the government's control.
- In August 1989, F.W. de Klerk became president of South Africa. He officially opened negotiations with the ANC to put an end to apartheid. on 11 February 1990, Nelson Mandela and the other political prisoners were released.
- In June 1991, the Population Registration Act and the Group Areas Act were abolished. This marked the end of institutionalised apartheid.
- South Africa's first multiracial elections were held on 27 April 1994 and won by Nelson Mandela. On the same day, the Bantustans were officially reincorporated into South African territory.

We want to hear from you!
Leave a comment on your online library
and share your favourite books on social media!

FIND OUT MORE

BIBLIOGRAPHY

- Barjot, D. and Mathis, C.-F. (2009) *Le monde britannique. 1815-1931*. Paris: SEDES/CNED.
- Braeckman, C. (2003) Paysans sans terre d'Afrique du Sud. *Le Monde Diplomatique*. [Online]. [Accessed 16 December 2016]. Available from: <https://www.monde-diplomatique.fr/2003/09/BRAECKMAN/10540>
- Bris, I. and Feuillatre, C. (1996) Introspection sud-africaine. *Le Monde Diplomatique*. [Online]. [Accessed 16 December 2016]. Available from: <https://www.monde-diplomatique.fr/1996/07/BRIS/5632>
- Cessou, S. (2013) Trois émeutes par jour en Afrique du Sud. *Le Monde Diplomatique*. [Online]. [Accessed 16 December 2016]. Available from: <https://www.monde-diplomatique.fr/2013/03/CESSOU/48841>
- Chevalier, S. (2010) Les "black diamonds" existent-ils ? Médias, consommation et classe moyenne noire en Afrique du Sud. *Sociologies pratiques*. Issue 20, pp. 75-86.
- Corrigall, M. (2010) Mandela revu et corrigé dans Invictus. *Courrier International*. [Online]. [Accessed 16 December 2016]. Available from: <http://www.courrierinternational.com/article/2010/01/12/mandela-revu-et-corrige-dans-invictus>
- Encyclopædia Universalis (No date) *Malan, Daniel François (1874-1959)*. [Online]. [Accessed 16 December 2016]. Available from: <http://www.universalis.fr/encyclopedie/daniel-francois-malan/>
- Fallon, I. (2010) Le jour où De Klerk a changé

l'Histoire. *Courrier International*. [Online]. [Accessed 16 December 2016]. Available from: <http://www.courrierinternational.com/article/2010/02/03/le-jour-ou-de-klerk-a-change-l-histoire>

- Fauvelle-Aymar, F.-X. (2006) *Histoire de l'Afrique du Sud*. Paris: Seuil.
- Fritscher, F. (2013) *Afrique du Sud. De l'apartheid à Mandela*. Paris: Le Monde Histoire.
- F.W. de Klerk Foundation (No date) *Homepage*. [Online]. [Accessed 16 December 2016]. Available from: <http://www.fwdeklerk.org/index.php/en/>
- Gastaut, Y. (2014) 1945 : l'UNESCO met le racisme hors de la loi. *L'Histoire*. Issue 400, pp. 58-61.
- Guyot, S. (2015) Essai de sociologie territoriale sud-africaine. *EspacesTemps.net*. [Online]. [Accessed 16 December 2016]. Available from: <http://www.espacestemps.net/articles/sociologie-territoriale-sud-africaine/>
- Hadland, A. (2010) *Mandela, une vie*. Paris: L'Archipel.
- H'Artpon (No date) *En bref, l'histoire de l'apartheid en Afrique du Sud*. [Online]. [Accessed 16 December 2016]. Available from: <http://www.hartpon.info/ht/?p=58>
- Houssay-Holzschuch, M. (1999) *Le Cap, ville sud-africaine : ville blanche, vies noires*. Paris: L'Harmattan.
- Jeune Afrique (2009) *Special issue*. Issue 20.
- Lebec, C. (2013) L'Afrique du Sud a mauvaise mine. *Jeune Afrique*. [Online]. [Accessed 16 December 2016]. Available from: <http://www.jeuneafrique.com/19311/economie/l-afrique-du-sud-a-mauvaise-mine/>
- Lebec, C. (2013) Négociations salariales à haut risque en Afrique du Sud. *Jeune Afrique*. [Online]. [Accessed

16 December 2016]. Archived version available from: <http://archive.wikiwix.com/cache/?url=http%3A%2F%2Feconomie.jeuneafrique.com%2Fregions%2Fafrique-subsaharienne%2F18564-negociations-salariales-a-haut-risque-en-afrique-du-sud.html>

- Mourre, M. (1996) *Dictionnaire encyclopédique d'Histoire*. Paris: Bordas.
- Nelson Mandela Foundation (2011) *"I am prepared to die"*. [Online]. [Accessed 4 January 2017]. Available from: <https://www.nelsonmandela.org/>
- Nobelprize.org (1994) *F.W. de Klerk – Biographical*. [Online]. [Accessed 15 December 2016]. Available from: <http://www.nobelprize.org/nobel_prizes/peace/laureates/1993/klerk-bio.html>
- Rivière, P. (2008) L'apartheid au musée. *Monde Diplomatique.* [Online]. [Accessed 16 December 2016]. Available from: <https://www.monde-diplomatique.fr/2008/04/RIVIERE/15826>
- Sean, J. and Foucher, V. (2006) *Afrique du Sud. Au-delà de l'arc en ciel*. Michigan: Michigan University.
- United Nations (No date) *The United Nations: Partner in the Struggle against Apartheid*. [Online]. [Accessed 16 December 2016]. Available from: <http://www.un.org/en/events/mandeladay/apartheid.shtml>

ADDITIONAL SOURCES

- Clark, N.L. and Worger, W.H. (2016) *South Africa: The Rise and Fall of Apartheid*. Abingdon: Routledge.
- Dubow, S. (2014) *Apartheid 1948-1994*. Oxford: Oxford University Press.

- Mandela, N. (1995) *Long Walk to Freedom*. London: Abacus.
- Mandela, N. (2011) *Conversations with Myself*. New York: Farrar, Straus and Giroux.
- Mathabane, M. (2006) *Kaffir Boy: The True Story of a Black Youth's Coming of Age in Apartheid South Africa*. New York: Touchstone.
- Stengel, R. (2012) *Nelson Mandela: Portrait of an Extraordinary Man*. London: Virgin Books.
- Tutu, D. (2000) *No Future Without Forgiveness: A Personal Overview of South Africa's Truth and Reconciliation Commission*. London: Random House.

ICONOGRAPHIC SOURCES

- Portrait of Daniel Malan. Royalty-free reproduction picture.
- Portrait of Nelson Mandela. Royalty-free reproduction picture.
- Portrait of F.W. de Klerk. © US Department of State.
- Photograph of a shop on the main street of a township in South Africa. © Heinz-Josef Lücking.
- Sign indicating that the beach and its facilities are for white people only. Royalty-free reproduction picture.
- Photograph taken in 1960 of Nelson Mandela burning a pass book. Royalty-free reproduction picture.
- Photograph taken by Sam Nzima of a student carrying the lifeless body of Hector Pieterson. Royalty-free reproduction picture.
- Nelson Mandela and F.W. de Klerk shake hands during the 1992 World Economic Forum. © World Economic

Forum.

FILMS AND DOCUMENTARIES

- *Last Grave at Dimbaza.* (1972) [Documentary]. Nana Mahomo. Dir. South Africa: Zephyr Films.
- *Classified People.* (1988) [Documentary]. Yolande Zauberman. Dir. France.
- *A Dry White Season.* (1989) [Film]. Euzhan Palcy. Dir. USA: Davros Films, Sundance Productions.
- *La Commission de la Verité.* (1999) [Documentary]. André Van In. Dir. France: Archipel 33, Entre Chien et Loup, La Sept-Arte, Radio Télévision Belge Francophone, Wallonie Image Production.
- *Catch a Fire.* (2007) [Film]. Phillip Noyce. Dir. France/UK/South Africa/USA: Focus Features.
- *Goodbye Bafana.* (2007) [Film]. Billie August. Dir. Germany/France/Belgium/Italy/South Africa/UK/Luxembourg: Banana Films, Arsam International, Film Afrika Worldwide, Future Films, Thema Production, X-Filme Creative Pool.
  Released in the USA as *The Color of Freedom*.
- *Invictus.* (2009) [Film]. Clint Eastwood. Dir. USA: Warner Bros.
- *Passé Komatipoort.* (2009) [Documentary]. Sylvain Sailler. Dir. South Africa: Zarafa Films, Zaradoc.
- *The Help.* (2011) [Film]. Tate Taylor. Dir. USA: DreamWorks, Reliance Entertainment.
- *Mandela: Long Walk to Freedom.* (2013) [Film]. Justin Chadwick. Dir. UK/South Africa: Pathé, Videovision Entertainment, Distant Horizon, Origin Pictures.

- *Zulu*. (2013) [Film]. Jérôme Salle. Dir. France/South Africa: Eskwad, Pathé, Lobster Tree, M6 Films.

SONGS

- *War*. (1976) [Sound recording]. Performed by Bob Marley. Kingston, Jamaica: Island.
- *Apartheid*. (1977) [Sound recording]. Performed by Peter Tosh. Kingston, Jamaica: CBS.
- *Biko*. (1977) [Sound recording]. Performed by Peter Gabriel. London: Charisma.
- *Nelson Mandela*. (1984) [Sound recording]. Performed by The Specials. London: 2 Tone Records.
- *Apartheid is Nazism*. (1985) [Sound recording]. Performed by Alpha Blondy. Pathé.
- *Nelson Mandela*. (1985) [Sound recording]. Performed by Youssou N'Dour. Magnetic Records.
- *Asimbonanga*. (1987) [Sound recording]. Performed by Johnny Clegg & Savuka. EMI.
- *Bring him back home*. (1987) [Sound recording]. Performed by Hugu Masekela. Warner Bros.
- *Mandela Day*. (1988) [Sound recording]. Performed by Simple Minds. Scotland: A&M.

MUSEUMS AND COMMEMORATIVE BUILDINGS

- Apartheid Museum, Johannesburg (South Africa).
- District Six Museum, Cape Town (South Africa).
- Hector Pieterson Memorial and Museum, Soweto (South Africa).

- Nelson Mandela National Museum (commonly known as Mandela House), Soweto.
- Robben Island Prison, Cape Town.

22523207R00030

Printed in Great Britain
by Amazon